SCOOP SNOOPS

SCOOP SNOOPS

by Constance Hiser

drawings by Cat Bowman Smith

Holiday House/New York

Library of Congress Cataloging-in-Publication Data

Hiser, Constance.
Scoop Snoops / Constance Hiser : drawings by Cat Bowman Smith.—
1st ed.
p.   cm.
Summary : When their neighbor is robbed on Halloween night, a group
of fourth-grade reporters decide to try to find the thief.
ISBN 0-8234-1011-0
[1. Mystery and detective stories.   2. Reporters and reporting—
Fiction.]   I. Smith, Cat Bowman, ill.   II. Title.
PZ7.H618Sc   1993   92-25922   CIP   AC
[Fic]—dc20

For Jeannie, who proves every day that
miracles really do happen.

C.H.

Contents

SCOOP SNOOPS

CHAPTER ONE

A Really Big Story

"Imagine, a real newspaper at Emerson Elementary—*The Emerson Bugle!*" said Paul VanGundy as he worked at the fourth-grade computer.

"You're the perfect editor in chief, Paul," said Nicole Clark, the sports editor, brushing the hair out of her eyes. "I can't wait to write stories about Pee Wee Football—and Little League next spring. Maybe I'll even write about the high-school teams."

"My first story will be about Roger Alberti's cat," said Nicole's twin, Michelle. "She just had eleven kittens—that has to be some kind of a record."

"My comic strip is coming along, too," Ben Rushmore told them. "It's neat, the way you can draw the pictures right on the computer. It's almost like being a real cartoonist!"

"You probably will be a cartoonist some-day," Michelle said.

Hank Lee, who would write the advice column, walked in and set a cardboard box on the table. "I put this box by the door so the kids could write to me with their questions, and it's already half-full!" he said. "Get a load of this one. 'Dear Bugle Boy, I was reading my sister's diary and lost the key. If she finds out, she'll smear me with honey and tie me to an anthill. What can I do?' "

"What did you say?" asked Nicole.

"I'm not telling," Hank said. "You'll have to wait and read the column."

Paul pushed a button to file his news story about the big spelling bee, then switched the computer off. "You know, guys, there's just one thing missing from *The Emerson*

2

Bugle," he said, swiveling his chair around to look at his friends. "We've got some great stories, but there's nothing exciting going on around the school. If we want to have a first-rate newspaper, we need something special—a story that will really make headlines."

"Maybe Pete Rogers will fall off the jungle gym again," Nicole suggested hopefully.

"Well, you can't count on it," Hank said. "Hey, I know—what about that flood in the basement last week?"

"I already wrote about that," Paul told him. "It wasn't all that exciting, anyway. The janitor fixed the broken pipe and had it cleaned up in a couple of hours."

"Jenny Ronson won the city spelling bee," Michelle suggested.

"It's on the front page already," Paul answered. "But I'm talking about something *really* big—you know, like if the president came to our school."

"Oh, sure," Hank snorted, "that's really going to happen."

4

"Well, it could," Paul insisted. "He came to Springfield last year, and that's only seventy miles away. We could at least watch the news and read the newspapers. All we have to do is keep our eyes open."

"How long do we have till the paper comes out?" Ben asked.

Nicole looked at the calendar by Mrs. Ross's desk. "The first edition comes out next Friday," she said. "And we have to have the stories done by Wednesday—eight days from now."

"We can do it by then," Paul urged them. "We just have to look."

"Maybe something will happen over Halloween," Michelle said. "At least we can write about the class party and everyone's costumes."

"Speaking of that," Hank put in, "do you guys want to meet at my house about six tomorrow night? We could go trick-or-treating together."

"Great idea," Ben said.

Just then the kids jumped as the bell rang

for the end of recess. As they scrambled back to their desks, Paul said, "Don't forget, guys—keep your eyes and ears open. There's got to be a big story out there someplace, and we need it for the front page of *The Bugle!*"

"How could we forget with you reminding us every five minutes?" said Nicole.

But as they took out their spelling books, the kids promised themselves that they would be on the lookout for a really exciting story. After all, they were the editors of *The Emerson Bugle*—and they were determined to make it the best newspaper any fourth grade had ever published!

CHAPTER TWO

The Trick-or-Treat Thief

The full moon was rising above the treetops as the kids gathered on the sidewalk in front of Hank's house the next evening. A frosty breeze nipped at their noses and rustled the dry leaves overhead. A fat, grinning jack-o'-lantern glowed from Hank's front porch, and the ghost he had made from an old sheet shone eerily from the shadows by the side-walk.

"It's a perfect night for trick-or-treating!" Nicole said.

The other kids admired her red-white-

and-blue track suit, Michelle's veterinarian costume, Ben's spaceman outfit, Hank's Superman costume, and Paul's business suit. "Let's get going," Hank suggested. "I can only stay out until nine o'clock. And I want to go *everywhere!*" Holding their treat bags tightly, the kids hurried down the block.

By seven o'clock, the bags were bulging with goodies—lollipops and candy corn and sticky brown caramels. And that wasn't even counting the chocolates and licorice whips and granola bars they had already crammed into their mouths.

"Look whose house is next!" Ben pointed toward the huge old redbrick mansion just behind the fancy iron fence. "Mrs. Calico always gives the best treats in town."

"And not just at Halloween," Michelle pointed out, as they pushed open the squeaky gate and started up the long side-walk. "Remember those chocolate chip cookies she gave us last summer?"

"And that delicious lemonade," Nicole

added. "She's nice, too. Mrs. Calico is one of my favorite people."

By the time the kids had reached Mrs. Calico's front door, their mouths were watering and their stomachs were rumbling, in spite of all the candy they'd already eaten. "I hope she has chocolate bars," Nicole said, as Paul rang Mrs. Calico's doorbell.

The loud chime of the doorbell echoed through the darkness, and the kids waited, grinning, for their friend to answer the door. Cutouts of ghosts and witches and pumpkins watched them from every window of the big old house, and the biggest jack-o'-lantern the kids had ever seen smiled a crooked smile from its perch on the porch railing. Mrs. Calico really knew how to celebrate Halloween.

"I wonder what's taking her so long?" Ben said a minute later.

"She's probably in the kitchen getting more candy," Michelle suggested. "Ring the bell again, Paul."

Paul pushed the button one more time.

But when there was still no sound of approaching footsteps, the kids exchanged worried glances.

"I hope nothing's wrong in there," Nicole said. "You don't suppose she's out, do you?"

"Not with all those lights on," Hank said. "Maybe she fell down. My great-aunt fell last winter and broke her hip. Old people do that sometimes. And Mrs. Calico's even older than my aunt."

"Maybe we ought to go in and see if she's okay," Paul said at last. "She's got to be here."

"Yeah, why would she leave on Halloween?" Ben agreed. "She loves kids to come trick-or-treating."

"Do you think we'll have to break one of her windows to get in?" Michelle asked.

"No," said Nicole. "Look—the door isn't even locked."

Sure enough, as Nicole turned the doorknob, the big front door swung slowly open.

"Mrs. Calico?" Paul called, sticking his head and shoulders in through the doorway.

10

"Mrs. Calico, are you here? Is everything all right?"

He turned back to his friends. "That's funny," he said. "No answer. But she's got to be here—she'd never go off and leave her door unlocked. Let's look for her."

"Be careful," Ben whispered, as the gang tiptoed in through the big front hall. "I don't like this at all. What if—what if there's someone here? Besides Mrs. Calico, I mean."

"Like a burglar," Hank mumbled. "Maybe someone's watching us right now. Paul, should we go next door and call the police from there? This could be dangerous."

"Shhhhh!" Paul held up his hand and cocked his head to one side. "Listen!" he hissed.

They froze in their tracks, straining their ears for the sound Paul had heard. A second later, the rest of them caught it, too—a faint thumping noise from the back of the house.

"We—we'd better see what's going on," Nicole whispered.

Hardly daring to breathe, the kids crept on

11

tiptoe through the old-fashioned parlor, down the long, gloomy hallway, and into the big, warm kitchen. The closer they got to the kitchen, the louder the thumping sounded. But the huge, cheery room was empty.

"Where is that noise coming from?" Michelle asked, huddling closer to her twin.

"Listen!" Paul gasped, pointing. "Someone's in the pantry!"

Sure enough, the sound was coming from the pantry next to the kitchen—and a kitchen chair was wedged under the doorknob so the door couldn't be pushed open.

Just then they heard Mrs. Calico's voice, faintly calling from inside the pantry. "Who is it! Who's there? Let me out, I tell you!"

"It's us, Mrs. Calico," Hank called back, grabbing the chair and pulling it away from the pantry door. "Hank and Paul and Ben and the Clark twins. Hold on, we'll have you out of there in just a second."

A moment later, the pantry door swung open to reveal a flustered-looking Mrs. Calico. Her gray hair was a mess, and there was a rip in the sleeve of her dress. But she was smiling as she greeted them.

"Thank heaven you children came along!" she said. "I was beginning to think I'd never get out."

"What happened?" Nicole asked, hugging Mrs. Calico. "What were you doing in there?"

"And who put that chair under the doorknob?" Ben demanded. "If that was someone's idea of a Halloween prank, it wasn't very funny."

Mrs. Calico sank weakly down into a chair by her kitchen table. "I'm afraid it was a lot worse than a prank," she told them. "Nothing like this ever happened to me before. I can hardly believe it myself, but—I think I've been robbed!"

"Robbed!?"

Mrs. Calico nodded, brushing a strand of hair from her eyes. "It was just a few minutes ago," she said. "I opened the door for a trick-or-treater—at least I *thought* it was a trick-or-treater. Whoever it was was tall and

13

CHAPTER THREE

Investigative Reporters

"Don't you worry, Mrs. Calico, we'll get your ring back," Police Chief Alvarez promised, when he had finished questioning the kids and making notes in his thick notebook. "I'm just glad no one was hurt. You're lucky these kids came along!"

"Isn't that the truth!" Mrs. Calico agreed. "If it hadn't been for the children, I'd still be locked in that pantry. I get dizzy just thinking about it!"

"We'd better be getting home," Nicole said, after the police had left.

"Oh, my stars, yes!" Mrs. Calico agreed. "Your folks will be worried. And tomorrow's a school day."

"They'll understand when we explain," Paul assured her. "And you know, Mrs. Calico, maybe we can help you get your ring back."

They all stared at him. "Us?" Ben said. "How could we help?"

"We're reporters, remember?" Paul said. "Part of our job is to investigate mysteries."

"But that's what the police are for," said Mrs. Calico. "They won't want you children involved. And besides, that thief wasn't just playing games, you know. You could get hurt."

"All I meant was that we could keep our eyes open for clues," Paul said. "For instance, if we saw someone wearing your ring, we could let the police know. And besides, Mrs. Calico, this is just the story we need for our newspaper. We've been looking for something really big for the front page."

CHAPTER FOUR

The First Clue

"I've got a great idea," Paul said at recess the next day. "I thought we could have a talk with Mr. Rush at the Costume Shop after school. That mask was so unusual—I bet there aren't too many like it. If Mr. Rush sold one of those, he probably remembers it. And if he remembers who bought that mask—"

"Then we're halfway to catching the thief!" Nicole finished. "Great thinking, Paul."

"And don't forget the drawing you did of

the mask, Ben," Michelle added. "That will come in handy."

The minute the last bell had rung, the gang headed downtown for the Costume Shop. Clattering through the door, they found Mr. Rush straightening the costumes that hung on long racks all over the shop.

"Hi, kids!" he greeted them. "How's your dad, Hank? Say, aren't you guys a little late? Halloween was yesterday!"

"We're not here for costumes, Mr. Rush," Paul told him. "We're investigating a crime."

"A crime!" Mr. Rush's mouth made a surprised-looking O. "That sounds serious! What happened, did someone steal your trick-or-treat candy?"

"It's a lot more serious than that," Nicole said. "Mrs. Calico on Maple Street was robbed last night, by someone wearing a Halloween mask."

"And since this is the only costume shop in town—" Hank added.

"Oh, my!" Mr. Rush straightened his

spectacles. "You mean, the mask must have come from my store?"

"Exactly," Michelle said. "We thought you might remember who bought it."

"It was a very unusual mask," Ben told him. "Here, I have a sketch. This is how Mrs. Calico described it."

Mr. Rush took Ben's drawing and studied it for a few seconds. Then he nodded.

"You're right," he said. "I do carry one style of mask that looks like this. I don't have many of them, though—they're expensive. In fact, I think I only sold three of them this Halloween. Here they are, on this table—see? They do look a lot like your drawing, Ben."

The kids shuddered as they stared at the ugly mask Mr. Rush held up. It was scary!

"Do you remember who bought the ones you sold, Mr. Rush?" Michelle asked.

"Let me think." Mr. Rush laid one finger beside his nose and closed his eyes. "I sell so many masks this time of year that— No, wait! I know! Mrs. Porter bought the first one about two weeks ago."

"Mrs. Porter?" Hank exclaimed. "The *preacher's wife?* What would *she* want with a mask like that?"

"I wondered the same thing," Mr. Rush told them. "But she said it was for a big Halloween party the church was having for the teenagers. And the next mask I sold went to— oh, yes, that was Mr. Rose, the high-school principal. He wanted it to use in the spookhouse the band organized to raise money for their spring trip."

"The preacher's wife and the high-school principal," Ben sighed. "Neither one sounds like a very good suspect."

"Wait a minute," Paul said. "Didn't you say you sold *three* of those masks, Mr. Rush?"

"So I did," the store owner agreed. "I'm trying to think— Hold on, it will come to me in a minute. Oh, that's right! Mask Number Three went to that Kaminski kid—what's his name? Tony, isn't it?"

"Tony Kaminski?" Nicole frowned. "My big sister goes to high school with him. She says he's pretty nice. I don't think he's the kind to rob old ladies."

"Thieves don't exactly advertise," Paul reminded her. "And you've got to admit he sounds like a better suspect than the preacher's wife or the high-school principal. It's somewhere to start, anyway."

"You kids had better leave this to the police," Mr. Rush advised them. "You don't know anything about investigating a real crime."

"We're just working on a story for our school paper, Mr. Rush," Paul explained, "and we told Mrs. Calico we'd keep our eyes open. If we can come up with a few clues, maybe we can help out."

"Well, just you be careful. This isn't a game, you know."

"Don't worry, Mr. Rush," Hank promised, "we Scoop Snoops know exactly what we're doing!"

And before Mr. Rush could lecture them any more, the gang marched back out to the sidewalk, more determined than ever. They had their first lead on a super front-page story—and they were going to get Mrs. Calico's ring back, no matter what it took!

CHAPTER FIVE

Lovebirds

"Are you sure this will work?" Michelle asked. The whole gang huddled in the bushes across the street from the high school waiting for the last bell of the day to ring.

"I hope it does," Ben said. "We can't spend all our time on one story. I still haven't finished my comic strip. And Mrs. Ross wants to look everything over before we print the paper, too. We only have five or six days."

"I don't know what else to try," Paul said. "If we follow Tony around a little, we're sure to find out if he's up to something. And maybe we'll even see him wearing the ring!"

"Why would Tony be walking around with Mrs. Calico's ring?" Michelle said. "My big sister is best friends with Angela Bartucci, his girlfriend. Angela wouldn't date a thief."

"She might not know he *is* a thief," Hank pointed out. "Anyway, this is the only lead we have."

Just then, the end-of-school bell sounded, and a minute later the high-school kids began pouring out through the front door.

"Look," Nicole said, "isn't that Tony now? Right over there—the one in the green jacket."

"Let's go!" Paul said, scrambling from behind the bushes. "But remember—don't let him see that we're following."

"At least he's walking," Ben said. "And look, that girl who's with him—is that Angela?"

"Sure is," Nicole answered. "I bet they're headed for the Burger Barn—that's where all the high-school kids hang out after school."

31

"Let's go," Paul said. "We can decide what to do next once we get there."

The kids trailed Tony and Angela all the way downtown, keeping about a block behind and trying to act as if they were just window-shopping. The two teenagers were too busy holding hands and looking into each other's eyes to pay any attention to the little gang of fourth graders behind them.

"Mush!" Hank snorted. "You'll never catch me acting that way with any girl!"

"What girl would *want* you to?" Nicole said, and they glared at each other.

"Watch out!" Ben cried.

Hank and Nicole had been too busy arguing to notice a speeding car as it *whooshed* by the curb, almost mowing them down. The car roared down Catalpa Street in a flash of gaudy lime-green paint.

"I know that car," Paul said. "It belongs to Buster McNab. He and his brother live above the auto-repair shop. My dad says he's the craziest driver in town. He almost hit you!"

Nicole's face had gone pale, and Hank was

Ben didn't even sit back down. "Come on," he whispered, walking past them. "We can eat this outside."

The ice cream made the autumn wind seem even chillier, but they took turns gulping down spoonfuls of chocolate sauce and whipped cream while Ben talked.

"At first I didn't see anything," he told them. "Then, just as the ice cream came, I looked at Angela, and—I saw it!"

"Saw *what*?" Nicole demanded breathlessly.

"The ring!" Ben moaned. "Angela is wearing Mrs. Calico's ring!"

"What?" Hank gasped. "Ben, are you sure?"

"Of course I'm sure!" Ben insisted, nodding very fast. "It was just the way Mrs. Calico described it—a gold ring with a big, sparkly stone in it."

"I can't believe it," Nicole said. "I never thought it would really be Tony Kaminski. He always seemed like such a nice guy."

"Nice guy or not, I guess that proves

it," Paul sighed. "You never can tell about people. We'd better go talk to Chief Alvarez."

"Wait a minute," Michelle insisted. "Shouldn't we make sure Tony Kaminski is the trick-or-treat thief before we call the police?"

"You might be right," Hank agreed. "But we can't just walk up to Tony and ask if he stole that ring."

"Of course not," Michelle said. "But we need pet stories for *The Emerson Bugle,* right? And I happen to know Angela has a pair of lovebirds that would make a pretty good feature. If I called and asked, I bet she'd let us go over there and do an interview. That way we could get a closer look at her ring."

"That makes sense," Paul admitted. "As soon as Angela has had time to get home, let's call and ask if we can go over to see the birds. Who knows—we may be about to crack this case!"

And he scraped the last spoonful of chocolate sauce from the bottom of the ice-cream dish.

"I'm so excited that you're going to write a story about Romeo and Juliet!" Angela exclaimed, coming into her living room with a large birdcage in her hand. "I hope you'll let me have a copy."

"Of course we will," Paul promised. "Your birds will make a great feature for our Pets Page."

"First," Michelle said, taking out her notebook and pencil, "how long have you had Romeo and Juliet?"

As Angela answered Michelle's questions, her hands flashed through the air, pointing out Juliet's beautiful tail feathers and Romeo's shiny, curious eyes. The kids got a good look at the ring on Angela's right hand. One by one, they gave Ben a tiny nod. It looked like Mrs. Calico's ring, all right.

"Say, Angela," Michelle said casually,

"that's such a pretty ring. Where did you get it?"

"Oh, do you like it?" Angela smiled. "I just got it a few days ago."

Aha! The kids looked at each other.

"This ring is my inheritance from my great-aunt Grace," Angela explained. "She passed away last month. It is gorgeous, isn't it?"

Great-Aunt Grace? The kids exchanged puzzled looks.

"Is it a real diamond?" Hank asked.

Angela laughed. "Oh, no," she said. "A diamond that size would be worth a fortune. This is just a crystal, but it looks real, doesn't it?"

"Are you sure it's not a diamond?" Nicole pressed.

"Of course it isn't," Angela answered. "Why?"

"We just wondered," Michelle said lamely. "Well, I—I guess I have enough to write my story. Thanks a lot, Angela. We'll send you a copy of the paper when the December issue comes out."

Outside on the front walk, the kids dragged their feet.

"A crystal!" Hank moaned. "It wasn't the right ring at all."

"There went our big lead," Ben grumbled. "Now what?"

"I don't know," Paul said. "You don't suppose it really could be Mrs. Porter or Mr. Rose, do you?"

"The preacher's wife?" Nicole snorted. "The high-school principal? Get real, Paul VanGundy."

"We're right back where we started," Michelle sighed. "And we don't have the slightest idea where to look next."

Heads down, feet dragging, the gang slouched down the sidewalk, kicking at pebbles in their path. Being investigative reporters wasn't nearly as easy as they had thought it would be!

CHAPTER SIX

New Evidence

"I hated to tell Mrs. Calico we didn't find any clues," Paul said as they left the old woman's house. "She was so nice about it, it made me feel worse."

A half hour later, the kids were still feeling so disappointed and gloomy, they didn't even notice Mr. Rush knocking on the window when they passed by the Costume Shop. Then they heard someone shouting, "Hey, kids! Come back here—I want to talk to you!" Slowly, they turned to see Mr. Rush leaning out of his doorway, waving his arm at them.

"What's up, Mr. Rush?" Nicole shouted.

"Come here," he repeated. "I just found out something I think you kids will want to know."

They looked at each other and shrugged. Then with Paul in the lead, they turned and hurried back toward the Costume Shop.

"Come in, come in!" Mr. Rush urged them, shooing them through the door like a flock of chickens. "I was hoping I'd see you kids today. I think I've got important news for you—if you're still on the lookout for Bertha Calico's ring, that is."

They all perked up at that. "Of course we are," Hank said. "What is it, Mr. Rush?"

Mr. Rush stuck his head out the door again and looked up and down the sidewalk, as if he were checking to make sure no one was around to eavesdrop. Then he shut the door and joined the kids by the shelves where the masks were displayed.

"You know those masks we were talking

about the other day?" he asked in a low, quick voice. "The ones like the trick-or-treat thief might have been wearing?"

"Sure," said Paul.

"Well, I was taking inventory this afternoon, and—"

"Inventory?" Michelle asked. "What's that?"

"I was counting all the costumes left over after Halloween to see how many I had sold," Mr. Rush explained. "And when I got to those expensive masks, I noticed something very strange." He paused. "One of them is missing!"

They all gasped. "Missing?" Ben repeated. "Are you sure?"

"I didn't order a lot of them, because I didn't expect to sell too many at that price," Mr. Rush said. "In fact, I only ordered seven masks. I sold three, so that should have left me with four. But when I counted them this morning, there were only three on the shelf."

"Could one have fallen behind the counter?" Hank asked.

44

"Or been put on the wrong shelf?" Paul added.

Mr. Rush shook his head. "No," he said. "I've turned this store upside down looking for that mask. There's only one thing that could have happened to it."

Nicole's eyes were wide. "You mean," she gulped, "you think someone *stole* it?"

"That's what I think, all right," Mr. Rush said grimly. "And furthermore, I think whoever took the mask might very well be the same person who stole Bertha Calico's ring."

Paul groaned. "But if we can't find the mask owner, there's no way of finding the thief," he said.

"That's right," said Mr. Rush. "I'm sorry, kids. I'm afraid you'll just have to let the police handle this."

The kids left the Costume Shop with long faces and drooping shoulders.

"What a bummer," said Michelle.

"Right," Paul added, "now we've got *nothing* to go on."

45

"Wait," Hank said suddenly, "maybe we don't have to give up yet."

"What do you mean?" Nicole asked.

"Well, we still have Ben's drawing of that mask," Hank reminded them. "We could make copies of it at my dad's office, and then each of us could show the drawing to everyone we know. Maybe someone will remember seeing the mask somewhere."

They thought it over for a long moment.

"It's a long shot," Paul said. "But it's better than giving up. Why don't we go to your dad's office right now? Then we can get started this afternoon."

"Yeah," said Ben, "the sooner we get started, the sooner this mystery will be solved."

CHAPTER SEVEN

A Suspect

But by late Monday afternoon, all the kids were tired, discouraged, and almost ready to give up. They had shown Ben's drawing to dozens of people—their parents, their teachers, and all the kids at school. Now they were going from house to house, talking to anyone they could find at home. But so far nobody remembered the ugly mask.

"Why don't we split up?" Hank suggested, when they were just a few blocks away from Michelle and Nicole's house. "Ben, you and I can take this side of the street. Paul and

Michelle and Nicole, you cover the other side."

"Good idea," Nicole agreed. "Then let's meet at the end of every block to see if anyone has anything to report."

No one in the first block could remember seeing the ugly mask. Halfway down the second block, the kids still hadn't come up with a clue. But then, just as Ben and Hank started toward the next-to-the-last house on the block, they heard an excited yell from the other side of the street.

"Ben! Hank! Get over here!" It was Michelle, waving frantically from the sidewalk in front of a tall white house. "Hurry!"

Their hearts pounding, the boys ran across the street to join their friends on the front porch of the big old house.

"What is it?" Hank asked breathlessly.

Paul pointed toward the front door, where a bespectacled old man stood peering at Ben's drawing. "This is Mr. Frank," he explained. "He's almost sure he saw that mask on Halloween night!"

Mr. Frank looked up from the drawing. "Oh, my, yes," he said. "Uncommonly ugly, isn't it? I'm almost certain I saw someone wearing a mask just like this on Halloween night."

"Where?" Hank demanded. "Who? What was he doing?"

Mr. Frank shook his head. "That's a lot of questions to ask at one time, young man," he said. "And it was several days ago, so I'm not sure I remember all the details. But it does seem to me that it was about seven o'clock, or a few minutes before. I had just closed my car door, and was going into the Quick-Stop for some extra Halloween candy. That was when I saw him, getting out of a car parked next to me. He went into the Quick-Stop, and I drove away hoping he wouldn't come here."

The kids stared at each other. That wasn't much to go on.

"Did you notice anything else about the guy in the mask, Mr. Frank? Like how tall he was? Or what sort of car he was driving?"

A Suspect

Mr. Frank frowned. "No, can't say that I did," he said. "Except—yes! I do remember what his car looked like. It was almost as weird as his mask—the strangest lime-green color I ever saw."

Nicole's eyes bugged out. "Lime-green!" she gasped. "But that's—that's—"

"That's very interesting," Paul interrupted, poking her. "Thanks, Mr. Frank, that really helps a lot."

"You're very welcome," the old man told them. "Say, why do you kids want to know about that mask, anyway? Is this some kind of scavenger hunt or something?"

"Oh, it's a hunt, all right," Hank said. "And you might have given us just the clue we need. Come on, guys. We have some thinking to do."

Thanking the old man again, they headed back to the sidewalk and huddled under a leafless maple tree.

"Buster McNab!" Paul breathed. "Who else could it be?"

CHAPTER EIGHT

A Totally Brilliant Plan

Paul took a big sip of root beer and flopped down on the carpet in Nicole and Michelle's living room. "This isn't going to be easy," he said. "We're not sure that it was Buster at the Quick-Stop. And Buster's not the kind of guy we want to fool around with. What we need to do is prove that he has that mask. Then we'll be able to prove he stole Mrs. Calico's ring. But how can *we* get someone as big and tough as Buster to talk?"

"I don't know, but my big brother used to be in Boy Scouts with Buster, and he told me—" Hank began. Suddenly, he stopped, and a big grin spread over his face. "Wait a minute," he said. "I just thought of something. There may be a way after all!"

"What is it?" Nicole asked.

"Well," Hank explained, "as I said, my brother Pete is Buster's age. They were in the same Scout troop for a while. Pete found out something about Buster that practically no one knows!"

"What?" asked Paul.

Hank smiled. "Well, you see, the boys were camping in the woods one night, and a little ol' snake slithered into Buster's sleeping bag. When Buster noticed it, he did a dance in his sleeping bag, trying to get away from that snake. It must have been just as scared as Buster, because it bit him on the leg and wouldn't let go—if it had been poisonous, Buster would have been in big trouble. By the time the other Scouts finally managed to shake the snake loose, Buster's face was gray—and then he ran into the trees and threw up!"

"I get it," Nicole said. "Big, bad Buster McNab is afraid of snakes!"

"*I* don't get it," Paul said. "How does that help *us*?"

"Don't you see, Paul?" Ben began. "There's no way Buster's going to tell us anything about that ring—in fact, he'd probably knock us down if we asked. But if he's scared of snakes—"

"—and if we happened to have a snake—" Nicole interrupted.

"—like my pet snake, Hiss—" Michelle added triumphantly, scooping Hiss from his cage to hold him up.

They were all grinning now. "Brilliant," Paul said. "We can scare Buster into telling the truth. I just hope you're sure about this snake thing, Hank. I'd hate to find out your brother was lying."

"Trust me," Hank chuckled. "Buster's scared of snakes, all right."

"What do we do next?" Ben asked, as they hurried down the sidewalk. "We need a plan."

54

Suddenly, Nicole's eyes lit up. "I have a plan," she announced. "It's too late to do anything today. But tomorrow, first thing after school, let's get together here at our house, okay? And—"

The Scoop Snoops gathered into a tight little clump and Nicole began to whisper. By the time she was finished, they were laughing so hard they could hardly stand up.

"I've got to hand it to you, Nicole," Paul said, between chuckles. "You're a genius!"

"And how!" Ben agreed. "Ol' Buster will never know what hit him."

"Just as long as *he* doesn't hit *us*," Michelle pointed out.

Their laughter faded, as they thought about big, mean Buster McNab. Nicole's plan had better work, they thought. Buster McNab was big enough to squash them like little bugs if anything went wrong—and they still couldn't prove anything he'd done so far.

"Well, you've got your big story, Paul," Hank said. "But I think it would have been easier if the president had come to town."

CHAPTER NINE

The Chocolate Chip Trap

"Are you girls ready?" Paul asked, as the Scoop Snoops stood across the street from the car-repair shop the next afternoon. "Buster's brother ought to be at work now, so you'll have Buster all to yourselves. Got everything?"

Nicole nodded, straightening the red cap of her softball uniform. "It's lucky the Panthers are having their big cookie sale right now," she said. "Our living room is full of boxes of cookies."

"*And*"—Michelle grinned, patting her tote

bag—"I have our *special* box of cookies right here. Don't worry. We know just what to do."

"I feel sort of bad doing this to Buster." Hank shook his head. "He may be a bad driver and a bully, but we could be wrong about him. My brother says he's had a hard life."

"But we have good reason to believe he stole Mrs. Calico's ring," Paul pointed out. "And there are no other suspects. Besides, we're not really going to hurt him, just scare him a little."

"Remember," Ben said to the girls, "we'll be right outside in the hallway, so yell if Buster gets scary."

"And I'll be at the bottom of the stairs, so I can run to the pay phone in the Quick-Stop if I have to," Hank reminded them. "I can call my brother at work, or even the police if you need help. Don't be scared."

"I'm not scared, exactly," Nicole said. "But I'll admit I'm kind of nervous. I'll be glad when this whole thing is over."

"Well, it will be in a few minutes."

Michelle took a deep breath. "What are we waiting for? Let's go!"

Crossing their fingers for courage, the gang marched toward the car-repair shop across the street. Then they sneaked around to the back of the building.

"Wait till we find someplace to hide before you knock on the door," Paul whispered.

"I'll stay right here at the bottom of the stairs," Hank said. "I'll be ready to run the minute you or Ben yell."

Silently, Ben, Paul, and the girls continued up the narrow stairway and found themselves in a short, dark hall.

"There's only one door," Nicole said, pointing. "That must be it."

Ben nodded. "There's not much in the way of hiding places up here, Paul. You and I will have to stand on the stairs so Buster won't see us. I wonder if he's home."

"I saw his car parked in front," Paul whispered. "Good luck," he told Nicole and Michelle. Then he and Ben quickly tiptoed down the first few stairs.

Nicole raised a trembling hand and knocked softly.

"Louder," Michelle muttered, "he'll never hear that."

Nicole knocked again, a little harder this time. A second later, they heard the thud of approaching footsteps.

"Keep your shirt on," a voice snarled from inside the apartment. "I'm coming, I'm coming!"

The door flew open and Buster McNab stood on the doormat, a scowl on his face.

"What's this?" he growled, glaring down at the two girls in their softball uniforms. "Whatever you're selling, I don't want any."

Nicole pasted on her biggest, brightest smile. "You don't want any cookies?" she echoed. "How could anyone not want any of our delicious cookies?"

"Especially when we're giving away free samples!" Michelle added, opening her tote bag to show him the tempting stacks of cookie boxes.

"Free?" Buster repeated suspiciously. "What's the catch?"

"No catch," Nicole said politely. "We're selling cookies for our softball team, and we're giving all our customers free samples, that's all. Wouldn't you like a chocolate chip cookie? They're scrumptious."

Buster grinned. "Well, as long as it's free," he said. He stepped aside and motioned them into his apartment, his eyes gleaming greedily.

A moment later, the apartment door closed behind the two girls, and Ben and Paul exchanged anxious looks. If everything went right, they were about to catch a thief. If anything went wrong . . .

Buster's apartment was a mess. There were empty frozen-dinner trays on the coffee table, old newspapers piled on the floor, and rumpled clothes on the couch.

"Yuck," Michelle whispered to her twin.

"What's that?" Buster asked, spinning around. "What are you two gabbing about?"

"N-nothing," Michelle said sweetly. "How many cookies would you like to sample?"

"How many you got?" Buster snorted. "Why don't you just keep them coming, and I'll tell you when I've had enough."

"Okay," Nicole said, just as sweetly. "Here—I hope you enjoy them."

Buster ripped open the box of cookies she held out to him, and quickly stuffed three of the cookies into his mouth. "Not bad," he said, spraying crumbs as he talked, "not bad at all. Did you girls bake these yourselves?"

"No, we're just selling them," Michelle said, watching in amazement as cookie after cookie disappeared into Buster's mouth. How could anyone eat that many cookies? "But I'm glad you like them."

"I'll prob'ly even buy a box," Buster said between bites. "I used to play softball myself, and I guess I don't mind helping you little kids out."

"That's nice of you," Nicole smiled, but she was beginning to feel confused. Was *this* the terrible Buster McNab all the kids in

town were scared of? He didn't seem so aw-
ful, standing there stuffing his face with
cookies. Maybe Hank was right. Maybe they
were making a terrible mistake. Maybe
Buster wasn't the trick-or-treat thief after all.
Maybe—

"Hey," Buster said, gulping down a
mouthful of cookies, "you know what these
cookies need? A nice cold glass of milk.
'Scuse me, will you, while I go pour myself
some?" And he disappeared through the
kitchen doorway, cramming cookies into his
mouth as he went.

"I don't know, Michelle," Nicole whispered, as soon as he was gone. "I'm beginning to have second thoughts about this
whole thing. He doesn't seem so bad.
Maybe—"

But her twin's eyes were fixed on something across the room. "Look!" Michelle
breathed. "Over there. On the chair."

Nicole looked, and her eyes widened, too.
"The mask!" she gasped. "It's the mask from
the Costume Shop!"

CHAPTER TEN

Hiss

"See? That just proves Buster is the thief!" Michelle said. "We have to go through with the rest of our plan now. I only hope the boys can get help fast if we need it."

Both girls jumped as Buster came back into the room, a big glass of milk in one hand and the last of his free cookies in the other.

"Delicious," he said. "I think I *will* buy a box. Give me the biggest box you have."

Holding her breath, Michelle dug into her tote bag until she found the special box.

"Here you are," she said, holding it out to him, "I hope you enjoy this."

"Oh, I will," Buster laughed. "Thanks a bunch, cookie. That's a joke, get it? Cookie? Hey, what's the matter? How come no one's laughing?"

Quickly, Nicole darted across the room and snatched the rubber monster mask from the chair. "Where did you get this mask, Buster McNab?" she cried, holding it up.

His eyes narrowed. "What's it to you?" he asked. "What are you trying to pull here, anyway?"

"The mask!" Nicole insisted. "Where did you get it?"

Now Buster was scowling. "None of your business," he said. "I don't know what's going on here, but I don't like it. As a matter of fact, maybe I ought to teach you not to snoop in other people's business."

"Quick, Michelle!" Nicole pleaded. "The box—*now!*"

As fast as she could, Michelle ripped open

the taped-up end of the special cookie box, shoving it under Buster's face.

"Aaaaagh!" Buster screamed, climbing onto the back of the couch and flattening himself against the wall. Staring in horror at the little green snake that had slithered from the box, he roared, "Get that thing away from me!"

Quickly, Michelle snatched up her snake and held it in Buster's direction. Nicole whirled and ran for the door, throwing it wide open.

"The police just drove up!" Paul shouted as he, Hank, and Ben ran into the apartment. "We got worried because you were in here so long, so Hank went ahead and called them. What happened?"

Before the girls could answer, there was a pounding of feet on the stairs. Seconds later, several policemen rushed into the room, led by Chief Alvarez. "What's going on?" shouted the police chief. "What are you kids doing here?"

"Arrest him!" Nicole yelled, pointing at

Buster, who was still standing on the couch. Michelle was still waving the snake in his face. "That's the trick-or-treat thief! He stole this monster mask from Mr. Rush's shop, and he must have stolen Mrs. Calico's ring, too!"

"I don't know what you're talking about!" Buster whined, shuddering as Michelle's snake writhed and hissed. "I've had that mask for years."

"You're lying!" Paul shouted. "And don't pretend you didn't take Mrs. Calico's ring, too!"

"Step back, kids," Chief Alvarez ordered. "Leave this to me."

Reluctantly, the gang retreated to the other side of the apartment. Only then did Buster dare to come down from the back of the couch. His face was still pale, and he was shaking all over.

"What's going on here?" Chief Alvarez asked again. "We got a call that two girls were in danger in this apartment—but it looks just like the opposite to me. What are you kids doing, waving that snake in this young man's face?"

"Buster McNab is a thief!" Michelle cried. "This mask proves it!"

"I didn't take anything," Buster insisted. "I've had that mask since I was in junior high. And I've never even been near Mrs. Calico's house. I don't know what these kids are talking about. One minute I'm sitting here watching TV, the next minute these two girls come in pretending to sell cookies. And before I know it I'm on the back of the couch with a snake under my nose!"

Chief Alvarez turned to glare at the kids. "Is that the truth, kids?" he asked. "Did you trick your way into this apartment?"

"But he's the thief!" Paul protested. "We know he is! Mr. Frank saw him wearing that mask on Halloween night—the night Mrs. Calico was robbed."

"I don't believe this," said Buster. "Listen, kids, why don't you take that mask to Mr. Rush's Costume Shop and show it to him?

70

He'll tell you it didn't come from his shop. That mask is four years old."

Chief Alvarez picked up the rubber mask and turned it over in his hands. "Not a bad idea," he said. "Sorry to disturb you, Mr. Mc-Nab. As for you kids, you scoot now. You shouldn't have been here in the first place."

"But, Chief Alvarez," Paul begged, "can't we just stay and listen? We're working on a story for our school paper, and—"

"You heard me," the chief snapped. "*Now*. I want to talk to Mr. McNab for a minute, and then we'll head down to the Costume Shop with this mask. But right now I want you out of the way. Is that understood?"

"Yes, sir," they mumbled halfheartedly.

"I wonder if Buster really took the mask," Nicole sighed, as they dragged their way downstairs. "Maybe we were wrong—maybe the mask was his after all. I didn't get a good look at it. Maybe it's *not* exactly the same as the mask that was stolen."

"I bet he did steal it," Ben said. "Mr. Rush will tell the police that. Then they'll look in

Buster's apartment and find the ring, wait and see. And I bet they never would have known to look there if it hadn't been for us."

"Hey, I have an idea!" Paul said. "Let's go to the Costume Shop and tell Mr. Rush we found his missing mask. If we hurry, we can get there before the police do, and we can get his first reaction for *The Bugle*."

"Yeah!" Ben agreed. "After all, it was Mr. Rush who gave us our first clue."

"I can't wait to see his face when we tell him," Michelle said, as the Scoop Snoops rushed down the street.

CHAPTER ELEVEN

The Secret in the Jack-o'-Lantern

Five minutes later, the kids tumbled through the door of the Costume Shop, red-faced and out of breath.

"Mr. Rush!" Paul cried. "You'll never guess what happened! We think we found your missing monster mask."

Mr. Rush's mouth dropped open. "You don't say," he gasped. "Why, that's—that's terrific, kids. How did you find it?"

"We just asked around town till we found someone who remembered seeing the mask," Hank explained proudly. "When we found out the person with the mask drove a lime-green car, we knew right away it had to be Buster McNab. No one else in town has a car like that."

"So we went to Buster's apartment," Michelle continued. "When we pretended to be selling cookies, he let us right in. And there was your mask, in plain sight!"

"So we called the police," Ben finished. "They're asking Buster about the mask right now."

"Really?" Mr. Rush asked, tugging at his collar. He took a handkerchief out of his pocket and dabbed his forehead with it.

"He says he didn't take anything," Nicole answered, grinning, "but we know better. Chief Alvarez will be bringing the mask by later."

"They'll probably find the ring when they search his apartment," Hank said. "Who else would have it?"

"Yeah, we really scared him," Michelle said. "You should have seen his face when I pulled my snake out of the tote bag.

He jumped about a mile, just like this—"

Throwing her arms out, Michelle leaped backward. There was a sudden crash and a plastic jack-o'-lantern flew from a shelf of leftover Halloween decorations.

"No!" cried Mr. Rush as he sprang to catch the falling pumpkin. But he was too late. The jack-o'-lantern tipped over on its side—and the afternoon sunlight caught the flash and sparkle of the dozens of rings, bracelets, and necklaces that had spilled onto the floor.

"What's all this?" Ben asked, bending down for a closer look. "It looks like real jewels!"

"Of course they aren't," Mr. Rush snapped, stooping to scoop the jewelry back into the jack-o'-lantern. "They're—they're just cheap costume jewels I sell for people to wear with their costumes. What would I be doing with real jewelry in the Costume Shop?"

"Here, we'll help you," Nicole offered, and the kids knelt to pick up the litter of jewelry.

"Here's something you missed," Paul said, stretching to reach a ring that had rolled under a table piled with plastic pirate swords. "I can't quite reach—got it!"

Straightening up, he started to hand the ring over to Mr. Rush. Then his eyes widened as he got a closer look.

"This isn't costume jewelry!" he blurted out. "This looks just like—like Mrs. Calico's ring!"

"Nonsense!" Mr. Rush snorted. "Give it to me."

"Catch, Nicole!" Paul cried, tossing her the ring just as Mr. Rush grabbed the tail of his sweatshirt.

Nicole caught the ring.

"Why, you—" growled Mr. Rush, whirling to face her.

Seeing her chance, Nicole tossed the ring to Ben and bumped Mr. Rush's knees, shoving him off-balance.

By that time, Paul and Hank had grabbed the plastic swords, and for a moment they had Mr. Rush trapped behind the counter.

Then the shopkeeper's hand darted out to grab Ben's sweater. Shaking the boy the way a cat might shake a mouse, he pulled him behind the counter and roared, "Get back! All of you—or your little friend will get hurt!"

Shocked into silence, the kids slowly backed away, while Ben dangled white-faced from the man's hand, his feet barely touching the floor.

"That's right." Mr. Rush smiled, his eyes narrow. "I'd hate to have to hurt anyone. Now, Ben, you just hand over that ring. *Now!*"

"You—*you're* the trick-or-treat thief!" Paul stammered, staring into Mr. Rush's hard, cold eyes. "It was you all along! You lied about losing the mask, too!"

"No more talk," Mr. Rush ordered. "Ben, give me that ring!"

As Ben twisted and squirmed in his grasp, Mr. Rush bent down to wrestle the ring from his hand, while the rest of the kids watched helplessly. If they dared to make a move, Ben could get badly hurt.

77

Just then the sound of a slamming car door made Mr. Rush's head snap up. Ben became still, and everyone else whirled around, just in time to see Police Chief Alvarez walk into the shop, Buster's monster mask in his hand.

"Fred, will you take a look—" the chief began, then stopped dead in his tracks. "What's going on here?" he demanded.

"He's got Ben—and Mrs. Calico's ring," Paul said desperately. "He's the *real* trick-or-treat thief!"

Chief Alvarez stared at Mr. Rush for a long moment. Then he began to move slowly toward the pair behind the counter.

"You don't want to hurt anyone, Fred," he said calmly. "Let the boy go, and let's talk about this."

"No!" Mr. Rush cried. "You'll never catch me!"

Dropping Ben, the panic-stricken thief hurled himself toward the door to the storage room.

"Stop him!" Paul cried. "He'll get out the back door!"

But Nicole got there first, one sneakered foot thrust out in the fleeing man's path. With a startled yelp and a thud, Mr. Rush hit the floor, only to be grabbed a second later by a grim-faced police chief.

"Quick!" Chief Alvarez said. "Paul, run out to the squad car in front of the shop and tell Patrolman Firkin to get in here on the double. And tell him to bring his handcuffs. It looks to me as if we need to make a little trip to the station."

Chief Alvarez hustled Mr. Rush out the door to the police car. "Nosy kids!" Mr. Rush muttered, as he passed them. "Why couldn't you have minded your own business?"

Then Chief Alvarez called to the gang, "You kids will all need to go in for questioning, too. Patrolman Firkin will stay here while you call your parents." Mr. Rush sank into the backseat of the squad car, and it disappeared down the street, lights flashing and siren wailing all the way.

CHAPTER TWELVE

Front-Page News

"I can't believe how wrong we were." Michelle sighed as she typed the last line of her pet column on the school computer the next afternoon. "We were so sure it was Buster. And we thought Mr. Rush was trying to help us!"

"Some Scoop Snoops we are," her twin agreed, frowning. "Buster is really a nice guy."

"Yeah, I'm glad he's not still mad at us," Hank said, shuffling through Bugle Boy letters. "It's a good thing we apologized right away."

"*And* that we gave him all those cookies," Nicole added.

"Anyway," said Ben, "at least we solved the case. If we hadn't found the mask at Buster's apartment, we would never have led the police to the Costume Shop. If you ask me, we did a pretty good job, mistakes and all."

"Just think," said Paul, "thousands of dollars' worth of jewelry hidden in a plastic pumpkin. Last night, Chief Alvarez told me that some of that jewelry had been missing for months."

"No kidding," said Nicole, "and Mr. Rush seemed so nice—it's hard to believe he stole all those jewels."

"It's a good thing he was stopped," said Ben, "but I hope we don't have to work on any stories like this again. I felt bad about the way we treated Buster, and my folks were really mad when they found out what we'd been doing. They would have grounded me for a month if Chief Alvarez hadn't bawled me out already."

The others nodded, remembering the scene at the police station the night before, when their parents had driven them downtown to give their statements to Chief Alvarez.

"Still, it was worth it to see the look on Mrs. Calico's face when she got her ring back," Michelle said. "I can't wait to give her a copy of *The Bugle* with our big front-page headline. What a great story!"

"And we even made headlines ourselves. Can you believe all those newspaper and TV reporters who showed up to interview us? Imagine—the Scoop Snoops on the ten-o'clock news!"

"*And* on the front page of the morning paper," Paul said. "Speaking of which, we'd better get busy—we still have to get Hank's advice column typed in and set up Ben's comic strip."

"Not to mention our front-page story," Nicole reminded them. "I bet no fourth-

grade newspaper in history has ever had a scoop like this!"

"You're right," Paul agreed. "The Scoop Snoops really came through on this one! What are we standing around for, guys? We have a newspaper to put out!"

And a moment later the computer began to click, beep, and flash as the staff of *The Emerson Bugle* got to work on the biggest scoop ever.